T0199178

MOMMY WANTS HER BABY!

Story and Illustrated by:
MARY CATHERINE RISHCOFF

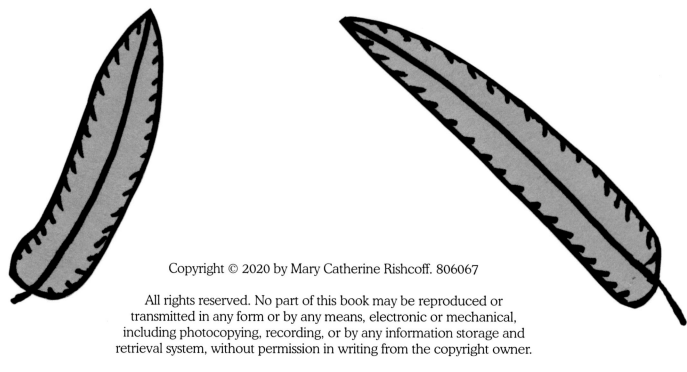

To order additional copies of this book, contact:
Xlibris
1-888-795-4274
www.Xlibris.com
Orders@Xlibris.com

ISBN: Softcover   978-1-7960-8934-9
        Hardcover   978-1-7960-8935-6
        EBook   978-1-7960-8933-2

Library of Congress Control Number: 2020903528

Print information available on the last page

Rev. date: 02/25/2020

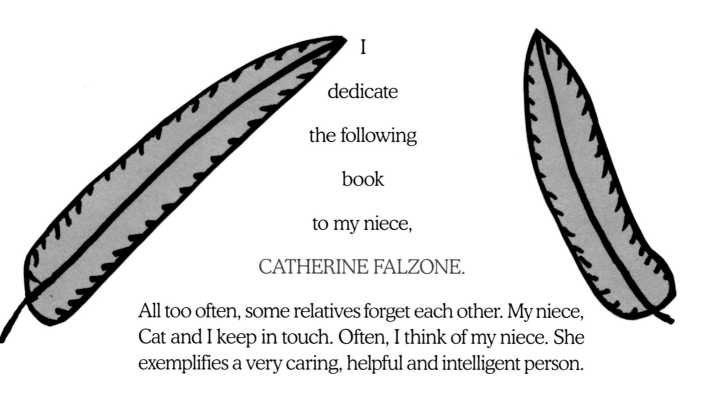

I

dedicate

the following

book

to my niece,

CATHERINE FALZONE.

All too often, some relatives forget each other. My niece, Cat and I keep in touch. Often, I think of my niece. She exemplifies a very caring, helpful and intelligent person.

Cat's life is filled with family, school, work, and with what I call her Zoo. Cat has pets of parakeets, a rabbit, a chinchilla, and a dog. Indeed, she is caring.

Cat taught me how to search on my laptop, which helped me to find publishers.

Regularly, Cat helps with household chores and the caring of my Aunt.

My niece worked in a pet store. She moved on to a big hospital. Also, Cat attends college. Her plans include medical school to become a pediatrician. Quite intelligent!

I appreciate all that my niece does, especially helping me over the years with her love and friendship. These days, we keep in touch with short, but loving texts.

PET STORE

Rabbit  Kittens  DOG

 PARROT

 Parakeet

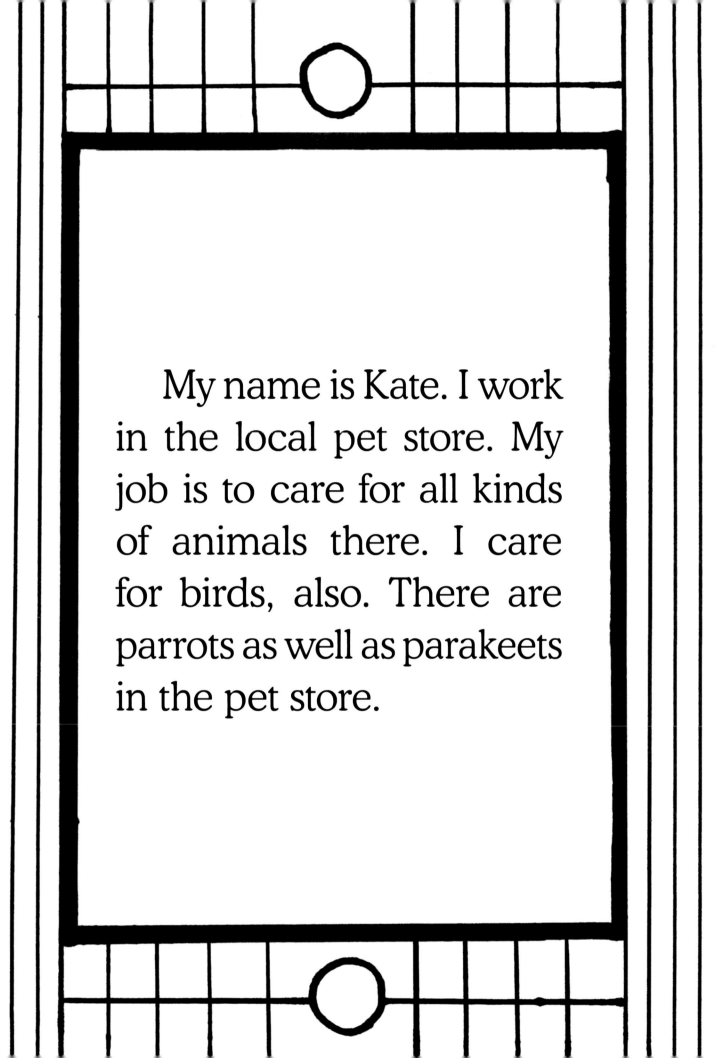

My name is Kate. I work in the local pet store. My job is to care for all kinds of animals there. I care for birds, also. There are parrots as well as parakeets in the pet store.

I met Sweet in the pet store where I work. Sweet is a parakeet. We got along nicely, so I fell in love with this particular bird. After a short time, I decided to buy it and to take it home. So little did I know!

Sweet adjusted to my home quite well. Sweet lived in a spacious cage located in the den. I got the bird several toys in order for it to amuse itself. Although Sweet thrived, something seemed missing. I pondered the situation. So little did I know!

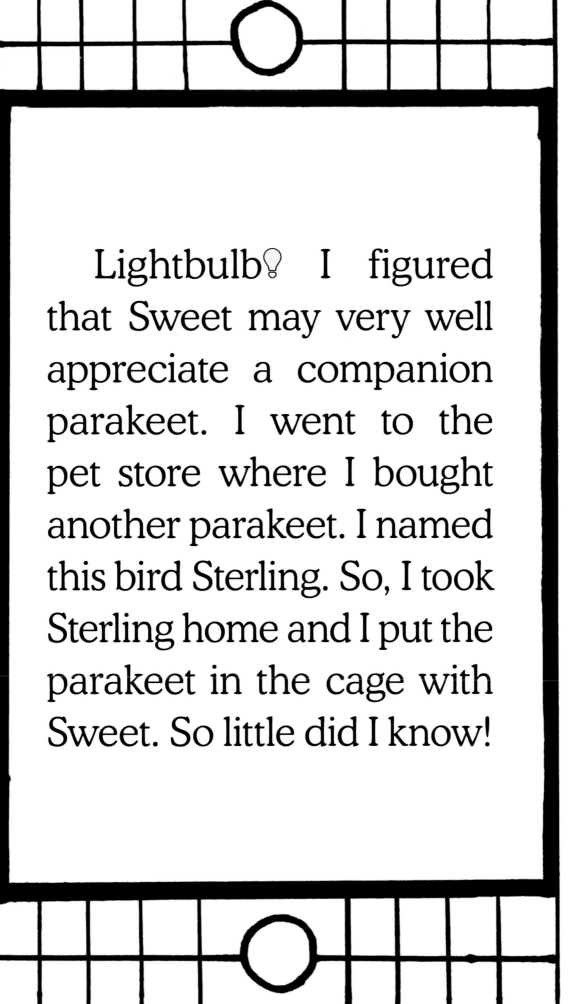

Lightbulb💡 I figured that Sweet may very well appreciate a companion parakeet. I went to the pet store where I bought another parakeet. I named this bird Sterling. So, I took Sterling home and I put the parakeet in the cage with Sweet. So little did I know!

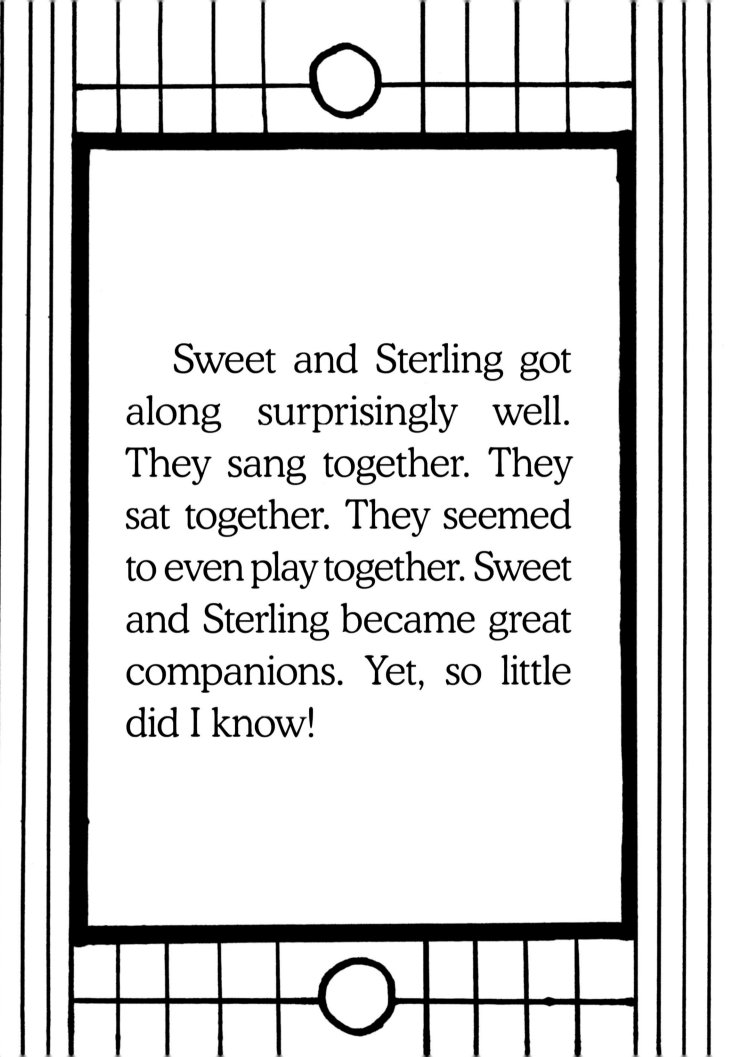

Sweet and Sterling got along surprisingly well. They sang together. They sat together. They seemed to even play together. Sweet and Sterling became great companions. Yet, so little did I know!

Soon it became evident that Sweet was a girl and that Sterling was a boy parakeet. I learned from my job. Who would think that the color of the cere of the adult parakeet distinguishes boy or girl? I learned that the cere is a fleshy covering. It is located above the beak on a parakeet. A blue or purple cere is a boy, whereas a pink or brown cere is a girl. I learned something.

Eventually, I saw Sweet peck at the newspaper on the bottom of the cage. Instead of singing, Sweet began to chatter. Finally, she dropped her first egg, but it cracked. Sweet dropped another egg, but I threw it away. Sweet did not stop at two eggs. She dropped a few more eggs, but none of these hatched. So little did I know.

To help Sweet, I put a wooden nesting box in her cage. Sweet dropped two more eggs, but in the box this time. Soon, one of the eggs hatched. The baby was her first. Unfortunately, it did not thrive. I was learning.

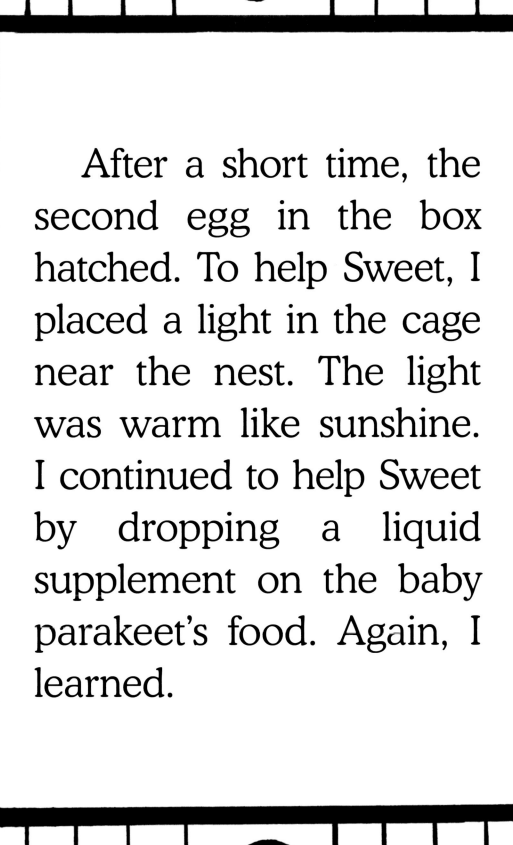

After a short time, the second egg in the box hatched. To help Sweet, I placed a light in the cage near the nest. The light was warm like sunshine. I continued to help Sweet by dropping a liquid supplement on the baby parakeet's food. Again, I learned.

The second baby parakeet thrived. It grew and grew from no feathers to lots of feathers. It grew bigger than Mommy. Sweet seemed content. She stopped dropping eggs and she continued to sing. Sweet had her baby at last.

I named Sweet's baby Sonny. It grew to be a boy parakeet. His feathers were yellow like sunshine. The extra heat given by the lamp saved his life. Indeed, Sweet deserved Sonny because she kept trying to the end, her baby! I learned.

Printed in the United States
By Bookmasters